The World's Best
Jinx McGee

KATHERINE APPLEGATE has written numerous books for young readers. She lives in Richmond, Virginia, where her household includes two cats, Bobo and Dude, both of whom claim to be the world's best cats. (Dude is still pouting because he appears in this book as a dog.)

Ms. Applegate, who also goes by the nickname "Kay," thinks "Jinx" is a swell nickname.

The World's Best Jinx McGee

KATHERINE APPLEGATE

Illustrated by Cathy Pavia

AN AVON CAMELOT BOOK

THE WORLD'S BEST JINX McGEE is an original publication of Avon Books. This work has never before appeared in book form.

AVON BOOKS
A division of
The Hearst Corporation
1350 Avenue of the Americas
New York, New York 10019

First Avon Camelot Printing: June 1992

CAMELOT TRADEMARK REG. U.S. PAT. OFF. AND IN OTHER COUNTRIES, MARCA REGIS-TRADA, HECHO EN U.S.A.

Printed in the U.S.A.

OPM   10   9   8   7   6   5   4   3   2

for Michael
the world's best

1

Just Plain Jinx

"On your marks, get set, go!"

Jinx McGee took off.

She knew she could win the race. She was the best runner in second grade. Maybe even in the whole world.

Jinx was even faster than George Bottoms. And George was the biggest boy in class.

She could hear the other kids behind her. Their sneakers squeaked on the wooden gym floor.

Jinx zoomed over the finish line.

"The winner!" called Wanda Moffett. Wanda was Jinx's best friend. She had red hair that grew in curlicues.

"Jinx is champ!" called Alex Starr. Alex was Jinx's other best friend. He lived next door to Jinx.

Alex and Jinx were the only kids in second grade who had an X in their names.

Ms. Sanders blew her silver whistle. "Group number two, line up."

Three more kids lined up. Wanda and Alex were going to race. So was George Bottoms.

Wanda and Alex looked a little nervous.

"Good luck, Wanda!" Jinx called. She crossed her fingers. "Run fast, Alex!" She tried to cross her toes, too.

"On your marks, get set, go!" yelled Ms. Sanders.

Wanda's curlicues bounced. Alex huffed and puffed.

But George Bottoms was in group number two. And nobody could beat George Bottoms.

Nobody except Jinx McGee.

"George Bottoms is the winner," said Ms. Sanders.

Wanda and Alex came back and stood next to Jinx. Their faces were red and shiny.

"George was too fast for us," Wanda said.

"That's OK," Jinx said. "You and Alex were the second fastest runners."

Wanda shook her head. Her curlicues jiggled. "I don't care," she said. "Running isn't my favorite thing. Violin is."

Wanda was the best violin player Jinx knew. She could play half of "Twinkle, Twinkle, Little Star" by heart.

"Running is OK," said Alex. "But reading is my favorite thing."

Alex was the best reader Jinx knew. He could read monstrous third grade spelling words.

"Running," said Jinx. "That's my most favorite thing." She bounced up and down on her tiptoes. She couldn't wait to race again.

Jinx watched the last group of kids line up. "Look who's in group number three," she said. "It's the new girl."

Jinx forgot the girl's name. It had something to do with money.

Penny. That was it. Penny Lawson. She had a long black ponytail that hung all the way to her elbows. And freckles on her nose.

"On your marks, get set, go!" shouted Ms. Sanders.

Group number three began to race.

Penny ran fast. Very fast.

Jinx bit on her thumbnail. Uh-oh, she thought.

Penny streaked over the finish line. She was the fastest person in group number three.

"That Penny is a very good runner," Jinx said.

"I'll bet you're faster," Wanda said.

Jinx grinned. She stood up a little straighter.

"Now it's time for the winners of each group to race," said Ms. Sanders. "Jinx McGee, George Bottoms, and Penny Lawson."

"I know you'll win," said Wanda.

"Jinx always wins," added Alex.

Best friends were nice to have, Jinx thought.

Jinx took her place at the starting line. Penny was already there.

"Hi," Penny said. She smiled. One of her front teeth was missing.

"Hi," Jinx said. She squeezed her eyes shut and tried to think about winning.

"Is your name really Finks McGee?"

Jinx opened her eyes. "Of course not. It's Jinx. J-I-N-X, Jinx."

Penny laughed. "Is that your real name? The one your parents named you?"

Jinx wished Penny would stop asking so many questions. "My real name is Virginia, but everybody calls me Jinx."

"How come they call you Jinx?"

Jinx tapped her sneaker on the floor. "My big brother made it up because I used to get into trouble a lot. But that was hundreds of years ago, when I was little."

"Are you runners ready?" asked Ms. Sanders.

George nodded.

Penny nodded.

Jinx nodded. She tried not to think about Penny calling her Finks McGee.

She tried to imagine whooshing across the finish line, ahead of Penny and George.

"On your marks, get set, go!"

Jinx flew across the floor. Faster than a race horse. Faster than a rocket.

George was behind her.

Penny was behind her.

Jinx ran even faster. She swung her arms. She pumped her legs. She almost forgot how to breathe.

She'd never run so fast.

Suddenly Penny zipped ahead. Her black ponytail flew in the air like a long black flag.

Jinx closed her eyes. Uh-oh, she thought.

When she opened them, she saw Penny whiz across the finish line.

Ahead of Jinx. Ahead of George.

Jinx came in second. George was last.

"Nice race," said Ms. Sanders. "Good job, Penny."

Penny grinned at Jinx. "You almost beat me."

"Almost," Jinx said. "But I didn't."

Penny smiled. The hole where her tooth was missing was big. Very big.

Just like a Halloween pumpkin.

Pumpkin Penny, Jinx thought.

"Maybe you'll win next time," said Penny.

Jinx felt her eyes get blurry. She stared at the floor. Her sneakers looked like they were under water.

She didn't want to cry. Not in front of Penny.

Especially Penny.

Jinx flopped down on the floor. "I have to tie my shoe," she said.

Even though her shoe was really tied.

Jinx knew she wasn't being a good sport.

She didn't feel like being a good sport.

She shouldn't have come to school today. She should have stayed at home in bed with the covers over her head.

Too bad. Running couldn't be her favorite thing anymore.

She felt funny without it. Like she had a hole in her middle and you could see right through her.

Jinx sniffled. She untied her shoe. Then she made a new bow and tied it even tighter.

She wasn't the world's best runner anymore. She wasn't Jinx the champ. She wasn't the best at anything.

From now on, she was just Jinx. Everyday, average, ordinary, boring, vanilla, second-best Jinx.

2

Jinx Thinks

On the way home from school, Jinx walked slowly.

Very slowly.

She walked like the slowest person in second grade. Maybe even in the world.

After all, running wasn't her favorite thing anymore.

"Hurry up," said her big brother Mike. "I don't have all day."

Mike was in fourth grade. He thought he was the boss of the whole world.

"Slowpoke," said Jinx's little sister Sara.

Sara was in kindergarten. She thought *Jinx* was the boss of the whole world.

Well, *most* of the time she did.

Jinx didn't answer them.

She was thinking about all her friends.
Everybody was the best at something.

Everybody but Jinx.

Wanda was the best violin player.

Alex was the best reader.

Maria told the best riddles.

Tyrone made the best drawings.

And now Penny was the best runner.

What could Jinx do better than anyone else?

She couldn't play the violin. Wanda had let her try once. It sounded like a very crabby cat.

Jinx liked to read. But Alex had read jillions more books than Jinx. Even ones with no pictures.

Jinx liked to draw, too. But sometimes her people looked like dogs. And sometimes her dogs looked like people.

And being the best runner was out of the question. Even if it used to be her favorite thing.

"Jinx, aren't you coming in?" asked Sara. "It's getting cold."

"Here I come," said Jinx.

Her dog, Dude, wagged hello.

Dude was the best tail-wagger in the world.

"Hi, Dude," said Jinx. She kissed his soft ears.

Jinx could hear her father typing. Tap-tip-tip-tap, went his fingers.

Mr. McGee was a writer. He wrote scary ghost stories. They had titles like *The Haunted High School.*

His books had too many big words for Jinx to read. But she liked the scary covers.

He was the best scary-book writer in the world.

Jinx followed Sara and Mike into the room where her dad was typing. There were crumpled paper snowballs all over the floor.

"Hi, guys," said Mr. McGee. "How did school go today?"

Mike grinned. "During recess I played softball and hit a home run."

"Terrific!" said Mr. McGee. "How about you, Sara?"

She grinned, too. "I got a star sticker for being the best counter in kindergarten," she said. "Want to hear? One, two, three, four—"

"We *know* how to count," Jinx said.

Mr. McGee looked at Jinx. One of his eyebrows jumped up. Then he said, "I'm very proud of you, Sara."

He looked back at Jinx.

Jinx looked at the floor. She kicked one of the paper snowballs.

"And what did *you* do today, Jinx?" Mr. McGee asked.

"Nothing," Jinx said.

"Nothing?"

"Nothing."

"You mean you just sat at your desk all day and never moved an inch?"

Jinx felt a smile start. "Almost," she said.

"Well, well," said Mr. McGee. "You *did* have an interesting day!"

Jinx went into the kitchen and sat down. She didn't feel like telling anyone about losing the race. Not yet, anyway.

Even Mike and Sara were the best at something.

It wasn't fair.

Sara came in and sat down next to Jinx. "Mike went out to play," she said. "Want to dress up Dude and pretend he's a baby?"

"Not really," Jinx said.

"Want to put diapers on Furball?"

Furball was one of the McGees' three cats.

"Why don't you ask Furball first?" Jinx said.

She wished Sara would go play by herself so she could be in a bad mood. It was hard to be in a bad mood when someone wanted you to put diapers on your cat.

Sara rubbed her chin. Jinx could tell she was thinking very hard.

"Want to put Barbie clothes on Floyd?" she asked at last.

Jinx sighed. "Why would you want to dress up a gerbil?"

"Floyd *likes* it," Sara said. "Especially the bride's dress."

"No, Sara," Jinx said.

"We could dress up Ed."

Ed was one of Jinx's frogs.

Jinx shook her head. Being an older sister was such hard work. "Ed's too fat for a Barbie dress," she said.

The screen door opened. Dr. McGee came in, carrying a grocery bag.

Just in time, thought Jinx. Lucky Ed.

"Mommy!" said Sara.

"Hi, girls," said Dr. McGee. She gave each one a hug.

"How was your day?" called Mr. McGee. He came into the kitchen and gave Dr. McGee a kiss.

"Busy," she said.

Dr. McGee was a veterinarian. She took care of all kinds of animals—even snakes.

"Did you fix any snakes today?" asked Jinx.

Dr. McGee shook her head. "No snakes today."

Jinx helped Dr. McGee take food out of the grocery bag. "You're the best animal doctor in the world. Aren't you, Mom?" she asked.

"Well, I don't know about that," Dr. McGee said. "But thank you, Jinx."

"Mom?"

"Yes, honey?"

"What am I best at?"

"Why, you have so many talents!" Dr. McGee said. She pulled out some bananas. Then she grinned. "How about forgetting to make your bed? No one does that better than Jinx McGee!"

"Oops," said Jinx. "I forgot again."

She always forgot. Jinx hated making beds. They always got messy again, anyway.

"Why don't you run upstairs and make it now?" Dr. McGee said.

Jinx headed for her bedroom.

Her mom didn't understand about being the best. She thought Jinx was joking.

But she wasn't.

She had to think of a new world's best thing to be.

Something. Anything.

She would just have to make something up. After all, there were plenty of choices.

There was scary-book writing. Or being an animal doctor. Or softball. Or counting.

Or even tail-wagging.

Anything but running.

Running was out of the question.

Jinx felt better. She would find something even better than running. She was sure of it.

After all, she had many talents. Her mom had said so.

At the top of the stairs, Jinx saw Sara. She was holding Floyd.

He was wearing a wedding veil.

Jinx could tell Floyd wasn't enjoying himself.

She was not surprised.

"Even Floyd won't play with me," said Sara.

Jinx smiled. She reached for Sara's hand. "How far did you say you could count, anyway?" she asked.

3

Jinx's Giant Bubble

The next day was bright and sunny. Jinx couldn't wait to get to school.

She had a plan. Today she was going to be the best at something.

Something new.

She felt her pocket.

It was there, safe and sound.

The package of Bubble Trouble bubble gum.

It was her favorite gum in the world. It was the best gum for bubble-blowing.

Jinx was a very good bubble-blower.

It was just one of her many talents.

Starting today, she was going to be the world's best bubble-blower.

Wanda and Alex were waiting for her at the monkey bars.

Jinx waved. She popped two pieces of gum in her mouth and began to chew.

"Hi, Jinx," said Wanda.

"Mmmmff," said Jinx. She chewed some more. Very loudly.

"You can't chew gum in class," Alex said. He was hanging upside down.

Jinx nodded. She already knew that.

"And it's almost time for the bell to ring," Wanda added.

Jinx nodded again. She knew that, too.

She held out her pack of gum to Wanda.

"No thanks." Wanda shook her head.

Alex couldn't have any gum. He was still upside down.

Jinx didn't have much time to become the world's best bubble-blower.

She mushed the gum in her mouth. She made it flat with her tongue. A nice gum pancake. Then she began to blow.

Very carefully. Not too fast. Not too slow.

That was the trick.

Mike had taught her that. Big brothers were good for *some* things.

The little pink bubble grew and grew.

"Nice bubble," said Wanda.

"Not bad," said Alex. He jumped off the monkey bars to watch.

Jinx blew some more. The bubble slowly grew. Soon it was as big as her fist.

It was a pretty good practice bubble.

Jinx sucked in her breath. The bubble slowly shrank, like a leaky balloon.

Now it was time for the real thing.

Jinx took off her mittens and unwrapped two more pieces of Bubble Trouble gum.

Alex shook his head. "Your mouth isn't big enough," he said.

Jinx just grinned. She popped the gum in her mouth and chewed hard.

Wanda giggled. "You look like a cow."

Jinx kept right on chewing. Cow face or not, she had work to do.

She chewed until the gum was nice and soft. Then she mushed it flat.

At last it was time for the bubble. The bubble that would make Jinx McGee famous.

Jinx began to blow.

"Here it comes," Wanda whispered.

The bubble looked like a bright pink egg.

Jinx blew and blew, slowly and carefully. Just the way Mike had taught her.

Soon the bubble was as big as a softball.

"Not bad at all," said Alex.

Tyrone ran over to watch. "That's an A-plus bubble," he said.

"Sure is," Wanda added. Her eyes were very wide.

Jinx blew some more. She still had plenty of gum.

The bubble grew even bigger. It wiggled when the wind blew.

It was almost as big as Jinx's head. All she could see was bubble.

Other kids gathered around to see Jinx's amazing bubble.

"It's as big as a basketball!" said Maria.

"Bigger," said Penny.

"Outstanding bubble," said Alex.

Jinx smiled. Alex liked to use big words.

It was hard to smile and blow a bubble at the same time.

"I blew a bigger bubble once," said Stan.

"It's true," Maria said. "I saw it."

Jinx frowned. This bubble had to be the biggest. No matter what.

Just then the bell rang.

Nobody moved.

Everyone was staring at Jinx's bubble.

"I'm going to pop it," said George. He stuck out his finger.

"No!" Wanda yelled. "It's too beautiful to pop!"

George dropped his hand.

Jinx blew a little harder.

Just a little bit more, and it would be the world's best. Bigger even than Stan's.

"What's going on here?"

It was Ms. Lambert.

She walked over to the group. Her hands were on her hips.

She had on her I-mean-business face.

Uh-oh, thought Jinx. Bubble time was over.

Jinx blew one last time. Just so Ms. Lambert could see her amazing bubble-blowing skill.

The bubble stretched. Then it wiggled.

Stretch. Wiggle. Stretch—

SPLAT!

Jinx reached up to touch her face.

Pink gum was stuck everywhere.

Her eyes. Her ears. Her hair. Her chin. Her nose.

Everywhere.

Everyone began to laugh.

"Hey, bubble-head!" said Tyrone.

"Now I see why they call you Jinx," said Penny.

Jinx sent Penny a mad look.

She did not think Penny's joke was funny.

Not even a little bit.

"Didn't you hear the bell?" said Ms. Lambert.

All the kids ran inside.

Everyone but Jinx.

"Did you forget our rule about gum?" asked Ms. Lambert.

She asked it in a soft way. Not in a you're-in-trouble way.

Jinx shook her head. "That's why I blew it on the playground."

Ms. Lambert smiled. "It was a fine bubble."

Jinx reached up to feel her hair. It was glued together in a gum lump.

"It was supposed to be the best bubble in the world," she said.

"And it was, for a little bit."

"Not the *very* best."

Ms. Lambert pointed to the door. "Why

don't you stop by the girls' room and clean up?"

Jinx followed Ms. Lambert inside.

She went to the girls' room and looked in the mirror.

There was gum everywhere.

She peeled some off her cheek.

Tyrone was right. She *was* a bubble-head.

Jinx picked some gum out of her hair. It hurt.

She was going to be in here a long time.

She was the best, all right. The world's best mess.

She was going to have to think of another best thing to be.

Bubble-blowing was way too dangerous.

4

Jinx and Jim

The next day was a no-school day.
Saturday.

Jinx looked out the window when she
woke up.

The yard was gone! There was fluffy
white snow instead of grass.

Jinx ran downstairs. She stepped onto the
porch in her kitty pajamas. Dude came, too.

Big wet snowflakes tickled her lashes.

Dude leaped off the porch and ate some
snow. It was his favorite thing to eat, besides slippers.

Jinx scooped up a handful and scrunched
it into a ball. "Perfect," she said. Just
right for building snowmen.

She tossed the snowball into the air.
Dude caught it in his mouth. He ate that,
too.

Jinx dashed back into the house. She got dressed as fast as she could and went back outside.

She and Dude ran around the back yard in big circles.

"Perfect," Jinx said. Just right for slip-sliding.

Then she remembered. Running wasn't her favorite thing anymore.

She remembered other things, too. Things like losing the race to Pumpkin Penny. And being a bubble-head.

Jinx began to walk.

Walking wasn't so bad, really. Not as much fun as running. But her feet made nice crunchy sounds in the snow.

Suddenly Jinx had a wonderful idea. A brand-new best in the world thing to be.

Easier than running. And safer than bubbles.

She, Jinx McGee, would become the world's best snowman builder!

Snowman building was just one of her many talents.

Jinx made a little ball and began to roll it in the snow.

It got bigger and bigger. It got heavier and heavier.

The ball picked up the snow on the lawn as she rolled. Soon there were stripes of brown grass where the snow used to be.

Sara and Mike came out. Sara had on her puffy white jacket.

She looked like a marshmallow. A marshmallow with feet.

"What are you making?" Sara asked.

"The world's best snowman," said Jinx as she rolled.

"I hope you don't run out of snow," Mike said.

"She could borrow some," Sara said. "From the neighbors."

Jinx kept rolling. After a while, the sky ran out of snowflakes. Jinx took off her hat. It was starting to get a little warmer. Icicles were dripping like melty popsicles.

Next door, Alex came out of his house. He was pulling his little brother Max on a snow saucer.

Max kept rolling off.

"Snowman?" Alex called.

"Yep," Jinx said. "The world's best."

"How big?"

Jinx thought for a minute. Good question.

"As big as Mike?" Alex asked.

"*Much* bigger."

"As big as that tree?" Alex asked, pointing.

"*Much* bigger."

"As big as your house?" Alex wondered.

Jinx thought again. Her house was pretty big.

"Bigger," she said.

"Outstanding," Alex said. "Stop eating snow, Max."

"Tell everybody," Jinx said. "Tell them to come see Jinx McGee, the world's best snowman builder."

"I will," Alex promised. He pulled on the saucer and Max rolled off.

"You forgot Max," Jinx called. Then she started back to work.

Jinx looked up at her house and squinted. It was taller than she remembered.

Maybe she could let Mike and Sara help with the snowman a little bit.

Just to be nice.

Also, she was getting sick of snow.

Then she thought again.

Nope. This had to be her snowman. All by herself.

Otherwise, she would just be part of the world's best snowman-making family.

"I'm going in," said Mike after a while. "There are good cartoons on."

"Me, too," said Sara. "My toes are frozen. Besides, Mom's making oatmeal cookies."

"Not me," Jinx said.

Sara frowned at the sky. "But it's getting cloudy."

Jinx shook her head. "My snowman comes first."

All alone, Jinx kept on working.

She could barely reach the top of her snowman now.

Her mittens were wet. Her nose was running. She kept thinking of warm cookies.

Dr. McGee came out with Sara. "Look what we brought," Sara said.

She handed Jinx two black lumps of charcoal. "For his eyes."

Dr. McGee reached into her pocket. Out came a carrot.

"His nose!" Jinx exclaimed.

Jinx reached up and gave the snowman a face. "Not bad," she said.

"Not bad," Sara said, too.

But there was something missing.

Jinx thought for a moment. Then she took off her scarf. "It's too hot for me to wear a scarf," she said.

She wrapped it around her snowman's fat neck.

"Very dashing," Dr. McGee said. "Does he have a name?"

"Jim, I believe."

Jinx stepped back. Her snowman was wonderful.

A little short, maybe. But nice and fat.

"He's the best," Jinx said. "Don't you think?"

"Absolutely," Dr. McGee said.

"He's smaller than the house, though."

"Just a bit."

Jinx looked around. "I want everyone to see," she said. "Alex is coming back with friends. Then they'll see I'm the world's best snowman maker."

"And the world's best sister," Sara added.

"I'm your only sister," Jinx reminded her.

"You could have a cookie while you wait," Dr. McGee said.

Jinx thought for a moment. Her stomach told her the answer.

"Wait here, Jim," Jinx said. She gave him a pat.

Then she went inside and ate nine cookies in a row.

After cookie number nine, Jinx looked out the window to check on Jim.

Rain had started to come down instead of snow. There was a little puddle by Jim's feet.

If he had feet.

I must have used a lot of snow, Jinx thought. Some places in the yard, it was all gone. Cement and grass had grown back.

She looked up and down the street.

No sign of Alex and Max.

Jinx sighed.

She went to the family room and watched TV with Mike.

He hogged the channel changer. And made her watch fat guys wrestling.

Finally the doorbell rang.

It was Alex and Max, with lots of friends. Wanda and Tyrone. Stan. Maria.

They were carrying umbrellas and wearing bright-colored boots.

"We're here to see the world's best snowman," said Wanda.

"The gigantic snowman," Tyrone added.

"Taller than your house," said Maria. "Where is he, anyway?"

"I thought he was in the front yard," Alex said. "Stop eating mud, Max."

Uh-oh, Jinx thought.

She peeked outside. Rain was everywhere. Mud was everywhere. Grass was everywhere.

Jim was nowhere.

Jinx got her green umbrella. Slowly she walked outside. Her sneakers squished in the cold mud.

Her friends followed behind her, squishing, too.

"Hi Jinx! Where's everybody going?" someone called.

Jinx turned around. It was Penny.

Pumpkin Penny.

She was walking on the sidewalk across the street.

All by herself. No friends.

She looked like she wanted to come over.

"Hurry and show us your snowman!" Tyrone said.

Jinx forgot about Penny. She had more important things to worry about anyway.

Like poor old Jim.

He was just two pieces of coal and a very wet scarf.

And a little snowball with a carrot in it.

"That's your giant snowman?" Tyrone cried.

Everyone began to laugh.

"Puddleman is more like it," said Maria.

"He *was* gigantic," Jinx said quietly. "And very dashing."

She picked up a mushy piece of charcoal. Her fingers turned black.

Jim was just a carrot snowball now.

Dude stopped by to sniff Jim's nose.

Then he ate it.

Jinx had been the world's best snowman builder. Too bad no one would believe her.

Too bad the rain had to go and ruin everything.

She would have to find a new best thing to be.

You just couldn't count on snow. It was very unreliable.

5

Lunch with Jinx

Monday, back-to-school day, it rained some more.

The snow was all gone. Jinx hoped everybody had forgotten about Jim.

Nope.

At lunch, Alex said, "That snowman was the best, Jinx!"

Jinx frowned. "You mean best because he was the worst."

Alex shook his head. "Best because he was funniest."

Jinx groaned. "He wasn't supposed to be funny-best."

She opened her lunch bag and made a face. It was egg salad.

Her dad always made egg salad. He thought he was a good cook.

He was the world's best scary-book writer.

But he was not the world's best cook.

"Want to trade?" Jinx asked. She held up her sandwich.

Egg goop dripped out.

Her friends shook their heads.

"Have half of mine," Wanda said. "It's tuna."

Tuna was Jinx's second favorite sandwich. Right after peanut butter and banana.

"Thanks," Jinx said. She reached for half of Wanda's sandwich.

"Jinx, you'll eat anything," Wanda said.

Jinx nodded. "Anything but egg salad."

"You have an outstanding appetite," Alex said. "Even bigger than George Bottoms."

Jinx looked over at George.

He was a big eater. He could eat two hot lunches and still have room for dessert.

Suddenly she had an idea. A wonderful, why-didn't-I-think-of-it-before idea.

She could become the world's best eater!

How hard could it be?

After all, eating was just one of her many talents.

Then she thought again.

Of her lost race. And her burst bubble. And her invisible snowman.

She was getting a little tired of trying to be the world's best anything.

It was pretty hard work. Plus, she kept choosing the wrong things.

Jinx turned to Wanda. "How come you play the violin?" she asked.

Wanda swallowed her last bite of sandwich. "I like it," she said. "Of course."

Jinx turned to Alex. "Why do you read so many books?" she asked.

"I like to," Alex said. As if it was a silly question.

Jinx thought for a minute. "I like to eat," she said. "A lot." She opened a bag of raisins. "I was thinking. Maybe I could become the world's best eater."

Wanda blinked. "Why?"

That was a hard one.

"To be special," Jinx said after a while. "Like you and Alex and Tyrone and Maria and Penny are special."

Alex looked surprised. "We are?"

"Of course," Jinx said.

She pointed to Alex's dinosaur lunch box. "Don't you want your carrot sticks?"

"I'm full," Alex said. "Here."

Jinx smiled. "Thanks," she said. She took a bite of carrot. "I am about to prove that I, Jinx McGee, am the best eater in second grade. Maybe even in the world."

She nudged Tyrone with her elbow. "Want to lend me some food?"

"You can have my cheese," Tyrone said. "I only took one little bite."

"Thanks," Jinx said.

She took the cheese. It had a half-moon hole in it.

"I'm becoming the world's best eater. But I need more food," she told Tyrone. "Pass it on."

Tyrone shook his head. "Jinx, you crack me up!" Then he nudged Willy. "Jinx wants leftovers."

"Here." Willy tossed an open bag of potato chips. "You can have the crumbles."

Jinx looked up and down the lunch table for more leftovers.

Desserts, hopefully.

And no egg salad. For sure.

Penny was sitting at the end of the lunch table. All by herself.

She was drawing faces in her applesauce.

Penny always sat alone.

She probably liked it that way, Jinx thought.

Anyway, Jinx had more important things to think about.

She didn't have time to think about Penny and her applesauce drawings.

"Are you sure about this eating idea?" Wanda asked.

Jinx looked away from Penny.

"You haven't even finished my half a tuna yet," Wanda said. She twirled a hair curlicue with her finger.

Wanda always did that when she was nervous.

She got nervous pretty often.

"Don't worry, Wanda," Jinx said. "Just watch me."

She finished Wanda's tuna sandwich in three big bites.

Soon lots of kids began to give Jinx food.

Fried chicken.

Peanut butter sandwiches. No banana though.

Graham crackers.

Chocolate pudding.

Strawberry yogurt.

Stan even gave up half his candy bar.

Jinx ate everything.

She ate so fast she wasn't even sure what she was eating.

People crowded around the table. They laughed and cheered and clapped.

"Go, Jinx!" Alex yelled. "The wonder mouth!"

After Stan's candy bar, Jinx stopped for a minute. She was starting to feel full.

Soon she was going to have to stop for good.

But the cheering was wonderful. She hated to stop.

Penny wasn't cheering, though.

She was drawing in her applesauce. Still.

Jinx was really starting to hate that lonely applesauce.

"Are you going to eat that stuff?" Jinx yelled.

Penny looked over. She seemed surprised. "You mean my applesauce?"

Jinx nodded. "Can I have it?"

Penny smiled her Halloween smile. "Sure."

"Bring it on over," Jinx said. "You can sit here, next to Wanda."

Sometimes she couldn't believe her mouth.

It was like it belonged to somebody else.

Penny gave Jinx her applesauce.

Jinx took a little bite.

To tell the truth, she wasn't feeling very hungry.

Her outstanding appetite was gone.

There was still lots of food left.

A brownie. Half a hot dog. A piece of celery.

And Penny's applesauce.

"Hurry up, Jinx," Alex said. "There's still more."

Just then the bell rang.

Jinx thought it was the most beautiful bell she had ever heard.

"Aren't you going to finish?" Penny asked.

Jinx shook her head. She didn't want to think about food.

Then she felt her stomach.

Uh-oh, she thought.

It was huge.

Like she'd swallowed a basketball. Or maybe a refrigerator.

"You look sort of green," Wanda said. She twirled a fresh curlicue.

Jinx felt sort of green, too.

She walked back to Ms. Lambert's room very slowly. Holding onto her refrigerator stomach.

"Jinx?" Ms. Lambert asked. "Are you OK?"

"She just ate the whole lunchroom," Tyrone said.

Penny looked worried. "I don't think she liked my applesauce."

"It wasn't your applesauce," Jinx said.

It was everything, she thought.

"Maybe we should go down to the nurse's office," Ms. Lambert said. "You can lie down a while."

Jinx nodded. That sounded like a fine idea.

She walked with Ms. Lambert there. Mostly she took little baby steps.

"Why did you eat so much?" Ms. Lambert asked.

"To be the world's best eater," Jinx said.

"You did pretty well."

Jinx shook her head.

She didn't want to be the world's best eater anymore. Not when she had to have the world's worst stomachache, too.

Jinx would just have to think of a new best thing to be.

She could forget about eating.

As a matter of fact, she was never going to eat again.

Ever.

6

Jinx's Big Surprise

By the next morning, Jinx felt better.
She still wasn't very hungry, though.
She'd probably never be hungry again.

Jinx hoped nobody at school would talk
about yesterday. She'd had to stay at the
nurse's for a whole hour.

She'd missed music, too.

Today was going to be better. Much,
much better. Thanks to her wonderful
plan.

It was show-and-tell day. Jinx could
hardly wait.

She was bringing her frogs. All six of
them. Ed and his whole family.

This was going to be the best show-and-
tell ever. And she, Jinx McGee, would be
the star.

Her frogs would be stars, too.

Frog-raising was just one of her many talents.

It was better than running fast. Or blowing the biggest bubble. Or building the best snowman. Or eating lots.

This time, nothing would go wrong.

Jinx ran down the hallway to class. Mr. McGee followed behind. Only he didn't run. He was carrying her big glass aquarium.

There was a towel over it. People couldn't see in. Frogs couldn't see out.

"Careful, Dad," Jinx said. "Frogs hate bumps."

Ms. Lambert was at her desk. "What have we here?" she asked.

"A surprise!" Jinx said.

Ms. Lambert smiled. "I love surprises."

Mr. McGee put the aquarium on the science table.

He peeked under the towel. "Bye, guys," he said to the frogs. "Try to learn something useful."

He kissed Jinx on top of her head. "Remember to keep the top on tight."

The bell rang. Jinx walked Mr. McGee into the hallway. It was full of kids.

"Have fun," Mr. McGee said. "I packed a good lunch today. Egg salad."

Good thing she wasn't hungry, Jinx thought.

She waved good-bye. Mr. McGee waved back.

Alex and Wanda ran up. "Was that your dad?" asked Alex.

"Yep."

"How come he was here?" asked Wanda.

"For show-and-tell," Jinx said.

Wanda looked surprised. "You're showing your *dad?*"

"Of course not." Jinx smiled. "My show-and-tell's a secret."

"I brought a new book to show," Alex said. "All about gorillas."

"I brought my violin," Wanda said. She held up her violin case.

"You showed that last time," Alex said.

"I know." Wanda looked at her feet.

"Maybe you could play 'Twinkle, Twinkle' again," Jinx said.

"I only know half," Wanda said.

"But it's my favorite half," Jinx said.

Wanda looked up and grinned. "Tell us yours, Jinx."

"No way." Jinx shook her head. "But I'll tell you this. It's going to be the best show-and-tell in second grade. Maybe even in the world."

All morning the frogs were very well-behaved.

Somebody croaked during spelling. Possibly Ed. But Ms. Lambert didn't notice.

Jinx could hardly wait for show-and-tell. Everyone was going to be so surprised.

Frogs were a very unusual show-and-tell.

Once Ross DeWitt brought a dead snake to show-and-tell. But Jinx's frogs were much better.

First, because there were six of them.

And second, they were alive, which was better than dead. No matter how you looked at it.

Right before recess, Alex leaned close. "I know," he whispered.

"Know what?" Jinx whispered back.

"Under the towel. You brought Floyd, right?"

"Better than Floyd," Jinx said.

Not that Floyd wasn't a nice guy. For a gerbil.

But there was only one of him.

And there were six frogs.

By recess, Jinx couldn't stand it anymore. She had to show someone.

When they lined up for recess, Jinx led Wanda and Alex over to the science table.

It wouldn't hurt to show them. Besides, the frogs were probably getting nervous. It was awfully dark under that towel.

"Just a peek," Jinx warned.

Alex looked first. "Hi, Ed!" he whispered. "Frogs were my other guess."

Wanda peeked, too. "Croak," she said.

Jinx lifted off the top. Just a tiny bit, so she could reach inside and pet Ed.

"Can I see?"

It was Penny. She leaned over to peek, and her long black ponytail swished.

"Nope." Jinx dropped the wire top of the aquarium. "It's top secret."

Penny looked a little sad. "Want to see my penny collection? I brought it for show-and-tell."

Jinx thought about Penny's lonely applesauce.

She didn't want to. But she did.

"Maybe later you could show us," she said.

Sometimes Jinx couldn't believe her mouth.

It was very unreliable.

"Line up, you four!" called Ms. Lambert.

Everyone ran to the door.

Outside it was muddy and cold. People were lining up on the grass to race anyway. Penny and George and some other kids.

"Want to race, Jinx?" called George.

Jinx leaned against the monkey bars. "Not today," she said. Not anymore, was what she meant.

Jinx looked away when the race started. Then she looked back. She couldn't help it.

Penny was winning, but it wasn't a very good race. Nobody was going very fast. Probably the squishy ground.

Jinx bounced up and down on her tiptoes.

Her feet still wanted to run. Even if her head didn't.

Penny ran over the finish line. George came in second.

Jinx kicked at a rock. She tried to think of Penny's stupid lonely applesauce.

But Penny didn't look so lonely right now. She looked pretty happy.

Penny walked up. She was still breathing hard. "I wish you'd raced, too," she said.

"How come?" Jinx asked. "You already beat me once."

"But you're more fun to race than anybody else," Penny said. "I ran faster when you were racing."

"You mean I'm more fun to beat."

Penny had to think about that. "More fun to race, *and* more fun to beat."

Jinx didn't say anything.

She wanted to say she could still be the best runner if she wanted to.

But she was pretty sure that would be a fib.

Penny was champ, after all. Fair and square.

Then she thought of Penny's penny collection for show-and-tell. Jinx smiled.

Frogs were much better.

They were alive, for one thing. Which

was much better than pennies. No matter how you looked at it.

Jinx couldn't wait until recess was over.

Pretty soon, she wouldn't be everyday, average, ordinary, boring, vanilla, second-best Jinx anymore.

7

Jinx and the Runaway Frogs

"Who would like to go first for show-and-tell?" Ms. Lambert asked.

All the kids waved their hands. Jinx waved so hard she thought her arm would fall off.

"Penny? How about you?" Ms. Lambert said.

Penny walked to the front of the room. She was carrying a paper bag that jangled.

"These are my pennies," she said. "Some are brand new." She reached into the bag and held up a glimmery one. "The oldest is from 1916."

Jinx smiled. Just as she thought. Frogs could beat pennies any day.

She looked over at the aquarium on the science table. The towel on top of it was crumpled at one corner. Had somebody been peeking?

Then she remembered. *She* was the one who'd been peeking.

"And this penny was made the year I was born," Penny said.

"Very nice, Penny," Ms. Lambert said.

"And this one—"

"B-R-R-R-R-I-P!" someone said.

Penny stopped talking. She looked around.

"Did someone just burp?" Ms. Lambert asked.

No one answered.

"Mark?" Ms. Lambert said. "Was that you again? You know it's polite to say excuse me."

"Excuse me," said Mark. "But I didn't burp."

"B-R-R-R-R-I-P!"

Jinx felt her stomach do a flip-flop. She knew that voice.

"Now who *was* that?" Ms. Lambert asked.

Jinx raised her hand. "It was Ed," she said.

"We don't have an Ed in this class," Ms. Lambert said.

Jinx looked around the room. Could Ed

have escaped? He was very smart, for a frog.

"He's sort of a new student," Jinx told Ms. Lambert.

"B-R-R-R-R-I-P!" said Ed. Very loudly.

"He's part of my show-and-tell," Jinx added.

"Maybe you should go next then, Jinx," Ms. Lambert said. "When Penny's through."

"B-R-R-R-I-P!" Ed said again.

"I'm guess I'm through," Penny said. "Ed keeps interrupting, anyway."

Jinx jumped up and ran to the science table.

Uh-oh, she thought.

The top of the aquarium looked a little funny. Like maybe she hadn't put it back on very tightly.

She took a deep breath. "Ladies and gentlemen," she said. "Introducing the world's best show-and-tell. My frog collection."

Jinx pulled off the towel.

She waited.

It was very quiet.

"You forgot to say they were invisible frogs," Tyrone yelled.

Everyone began to laugh.

Jinx looked inside the aquarium. The frogs were gone. All six of them.

"B-R-R-R-I-P!" said Ed. Wherever he was.

Ed and the gang were on the loose!

"UUGHH!" screamed Megan. "There's a frog under my chair!"

"B-R-R-R-I-P! B-R-R-R-I-P!" said Ed.

He sounded a little nervous.

"I'm coming, Ed!" Jinx cried. She scooted across the room and dived under Megan's chair.

But Ed wasn't ready to go back. He wanted to explore a little first.

With one giant hop, he headed for the door.

"Gross!" yelled Amanda.

"Yuck!" screamed David.

"Outstanding!" cheered Alex. "Go, Ed!"

"Jinx!" Ms. Lambert said. "What on earth is going on here?"

It was possible Ms. Lambert didn't like surprises after all.

Not this kind, anyway.

Jinx climbed out from under Megan's chair and brushed off her knees.

"Hey!" Tyrone yelled. "There's a frog by the window!"

Jinx turned. "That's Vince," she said. "Grab him, Tyrone!"

Tyrone dashed for the window. Vince looked at Tyrone and blinked. Then he hopped away.

"Stop, Vince!" Jinx cried.

"There's one under Ms. Lambert's desk!" Stan yelled.

"I see one, too!" Maria screamed.

"Jinx," Ms. Lambert said as she fished under her desk. "Just exactly how many frogs did you bring to show-and-tell?"

"Six," Jinx said quietly.

"Six?"

"Ed, Georgette, Vince, Carla, Pierre, and Ruby."

Ms. Lambert stood. She put her hands on her hips. "All right, class," she said. "Let's go on a frog hunt."

Everybody jumped up and began to search.

Everybody except Amanda and David.

They did their spelling instead, since they thought frogs were slimy.

"Jinx!" Penny cried. "Ed went into the hallway!"

Jinx dashed for the door.

"Come right back, girls," Ms. Lambert said. "As soon as you catch Ed."

Penny pointed down the hall. "There he goes!" she said to Jinx.

Ed hopped down the empty hallway as if he knew where he was going.

"He's probably heading to the lunchroom," Jinx said. "Ed has a big appetite."

She tore down the hall after Ed. He turned the corner and disappeared.

Suddenly Jinx ran into something soft that grunted.

It was the principal's stomach.

"What's our rule about running in the hallway?" Mr. Briggs asked.

"Don't," Jinx answered, trying to catch her breath.

"But we have an emergency," Penny said.

"Emergency?" Mr. Briggs asked.

"Runaway frog," Jinx explained.

"I see." Mr. Briggs tapped his finger on

his chin. "What exactly did this runaway frog look like?"

"Green," Penny said. "With big feet."

"And black eyes," Jinx added. "He's very handsome."

"I just saw a frog that fits that description," Mr. Briggs said. "I let him outside."

"Outside?" Jinx cried.

"I thought he was an outdoor frog who sneaked in after recess," said Mr. Briggs.

"We've got to find him!" Penny cried.

"I'll go with you," Mr. Briggs said. "I'm really very sorry. He didn't tell me he was from Ms. Lambert's class."

Mr. Briggs led Jinx and Penny to the door. "He went that way," he said, pointing.

"Ed!" Jinx called.

"There!" Penny cried. "I saw a green thing in the air. Probably Ed hopping. Or else a fat green bird."

"Let's go!" Jinx cried, and she took off.

"Careful of that mud, girls!" Mr. Briggs called.

Jinx dashed across the muddy field. Penny was right next to her.

Ed was hopping away fast, like he wanted to go home.

Jinx couldn't blame him. He'd had a rough day.

Jinx and Penny kept running. Their shoes made slurpy sounds in the mud.

Jinx had never run so fast.

It seemed like forever since the last time she had run.

Now she remembered why it had been her favorite thing to do.

Penny was breathing hard. Her flag ponytail swished in the wind.

She was just a few inches ahead of Jinx.

Jinx pumped her legs a little harder.

She and Penny were even.

Then Jinx was ahead.

Then Penny.

Then Jinx forgot to see who was ahead.

All she could think of was how she was flying through the air.

Like a race car. Or a rocket.

Like the fastest runner in the whole wide world.

Then she saw Ed.

"There he is!" she cried. "By that mud puddle!"

Jinx dove for Ed.

Penny dove for Ed.

Both girls landed in the mud puddle.

There was mud everywhere. Mostly on Penny and Jinx.

Ed, too. But he didn't mind.

Ed jumped into Penny's muddy lap.

"Hi, Ed," she said.

"B-R-R-R-I-P!" said Ed.

He looked a little guilty.

Penny looked at Jinx. "Nice frog."

"He's very talented," Jinx said.

Penny handed him to Jinx. "Also muddy."

"So are you, mudhead!"

"Me? How about you?"

Jinx looked down. Penny had a point.

"Good race," Penny said.

"Who won?" Jinx wondered.

Penny shook her head. "Search me."

"B-R-R-R-I-P!" said Ed.

"We better go in," said Penny. "Mr. Briggs is waiting."

Jinx gave Ed a pat.

It wasn't his fault show-and-tell was ruined.

He was just trying to have some fun.

She would have to find a new best thing to be.

You just couldn't count on frogs.
They weren't very well-behaved.
She started walking with Penny.
"Good race," Jinx said.
Sometimes her mouth amazed her.

8

The One-and-Only Jinx

When Jinx woke up the next morning, she had a cold. The kind with lots of sniffles.

"No school today," Mr. McGee said.

"But I *want* to go to school!" Jinx said, sniffling.

"Sorry." Mr. McGee shook his head. "Not until your cold's better. Maybe tomorrow."

Jinx flopped back on her pillow. "I know how I got this stupid cold," she said.

"How?"

"Chasing Ed. Penny and I got soaked." She sighed. "That was the worst show-and-tell ever. There were frogs everywhere."

"At least you found them all," Mr. McGee said. "And it sounds like Ed had a good time. But maybe next time you should bring Floyd."

Jinx shook her head. Then she sneezed.

"There isn't going to be a next time," she said. "No more show-and-tell. No more running. No more bubbles. No more snowmen. No more eating gobs of food."

"I guess you don't want any pancakes, then."

"I can eat, a little. Just not gobs."

"Why were you eating gobs?" Mr. McGee asked.

"I wanted to be the world's best eater. Alex says I have an outstanding appetite."

"Alex is correct." Mr. McGee smiled. "Of course, you're outstanding in lots of ways."

Jinx sighed. "Thanks, Dad," she said.

Dads had to say that. Moms, too.

It was some kind of rule.

Mr. McGee didn't understand that she was an everyday, average, ordinary, boring, vanilla, second-best kind of daughter.

"Can I lie on the couch and watch TV?"

"Sure," Mr. McGee said. "While I make the world's best pancakes."

Jinx smiled. "Dad," she said. "You are the world's best dad. Also the best scary-book writer. But Mom makes better pancakes."

Mr. McGee laughed.

After breakfast, there were a lot of left-over pancakes.

Mr. McGee gave them all to Dude. "Here, slipper-breath," he said. "Enjoy."

When Dude had finished eating, he and Jinx lay on the couch and watched boring TV together.

Then Jinx took a nap.

Then she read a book.

Then she watched boring TV.

And read another book.

Colds were no fun. That was for sure.

She missed being at school. Today was art day, too.

She missed Alex and Wanda. And Ms. Lambert.

And even Penny, just a little. She wasn't so bad, really.

Tomorrow would be gym day. She wondered if she would be all better by then.

There was something else Jinx missed.

She closed her eyes and thought about it.

Running.

She thought about whooshing through the muddy field to catch Ed yesterday.

69

Ahead of Penny.

Or maybe not.

Had she been winning?

Jinx couldn't really remember. All she remembered was zooming through the mud.

Funny. It didn't really seem to matter.

The doorbell rang. Two times.

Jinx heard her dad open the door. She heard voices, too.

Friend voices.

"Jinx? You have some visitors."

Jinx hopped off the couch.

It was Wanda and Alex and Tyrone and Stan and Maria and Penny.

Penny and Wanda were carrying something very big. Made of paper.

"What's that?" Jinx asked.

"For you," Alex said. "The world's biggest get-well card. It's gargantuan." He smiled. "That's my new word."

"We made it," Wanda added.

"During art," Penny said.

Jinx reached for the card. It was a big piece of poster board, folded in half. There was glitter on the front. And pictures.

Someone had drawn a smiling frog. He was wearing sneakers.

"That's Ed," said Tyrone.

Jinx read the writing. "Get Well Soon, Jinx!" it said.

Then she opened it.

There was more writing inside.

Everybody had signed the card. Even Ms. Lambert.

There was something else, too. More writing.

"You're the World's Best!" Jinx read.

She looked up. Everyone was smiling.

Jinx read it again.

She had to ask.

"World's best *what?*" she said.

Penny looked at Wanda, who looked at Tyrone, who looked at Maria, who looked at Alex.

"I'm not the world's best anything," Jinx said quietly.

Finally Penny spoke. "All I know is, when you're not around, class is *awfully* boring," she said. "In my old school, we never had a Jinx McGee. There's only one person in the world like you, Jinx."

Jinx thought hard.

71

There was only one Jinx McGee in the world.

She was it.

Then she had to be the world's best, didn't she?

The world's best Jinx McGee.

She wasn't everyday, average, ordinary, boring, vanilla, second-best Jinx.

Not anymore!

Jinx looked at her gargantuan get-well card and smiled.

Best friends were nice to have, she thought.

"Are you coming back?" Alex asked. "To school tomorrow?"

"It's gym," Penny said. "I hope you're all better."

"Me, too," Jinx said.

"You're the most fun to race," Penny said. She grinned. "And to beat."

Jinx laughed. "Just wait," she said.

She bounced up and down on her tiptoes. She couldn't wait to race again.

After all, running was her favorite thing in the world.

It was just one of her many talents.

Look for More Mystery Adventure
And Fun in the Kitchen With

Cookie McCorkle...

AND THE CASE OF THE
EMERALD EARRINGS
76098-3/$2.95 US/$3.50 Can

AND THE CASE OF THE
KING'S GHOST
76350-8/$2.99 US/$3.50 Can

AND THE CASE OF THE
MISSING CASTLE
76348-6/$2.99 US/$3.50 Can

AND THE CASE OF THE
POLKA-DOT SAFECRACKER
76099-1/$2.95 US/$3.50 Can

Each Book Includes Easy-to-Follow Recipes
For Cookie's Favorite Dishes!